A frog spends its life leaping out of the way of predators. But the stranger still seemed in a state of shock. He opened his mouth and his tongue fell out.

"What's the matter with your tongue?" I said. "Snap it back inside quick."

He pulled his tongue back into his mouth awkwardly, as if he wasn't used to doing this dozens of times a day.

"That's better." I looked him over. "You're a handsome green frog."

"Fawg," he said.

"Fawg?" I thought that over. "Did you say fawg?*"*

"Am I a fawg?" he said louder.

"Are you a fawg? Oh, are you a frog?*" I shut my mouth and waited. I'd never heard an adult frog ask such a question before. I mean, sure, tadpoles ask it all the time: Am I a frog yet? Am I a frog yet? But this fellow's body was almost twice as long as mine. His tadpole days were a distant memory. I spoke carefully. "Yes, you are a frog." I swallowed. "And a very fine one."*

He hung his head. "I'm a fawg."

→ **Donna Jo Napoli** ←

THE PRINCE
of THE POND

Otherwise Known As
DE FAWG PIN

→ ILLUSTRATED BY ←

Judith Byron Schachner

PUFFIN BOOKS

PUFFIN BOOKS
Published by the Penguin Group
Penguin Books USA Inc., 375 Hudson Street, New York, New York 10014, U.S.A.
Penguin Books Ltd, 27 Wrights Lane, London W8 5TZ, England
Penguin Books Australia Ltd, Ringwood, Victoria, Australia
Penguin Books Canada Ltd, 10 Alcorn Avenue, Toronto, Ontario, Canada M4V 3B2
Penguin Books (N.Z.) Ltd, 182-190 Wairau Road, Auckland 10, New Zealand

Penguin Books Ltd, Registered Offices: Harmondsworth, Middlesex, England

First published in the United States of America by Dutton Children's Books,
a division of Penguin Books USA Inc., 1992
Published in Puffin Books, 1994

20 19 18

THE LIBRARY OF CONGRESS HAS CATALOGED THE DUTTON EDITION AS FOLLOWS:
Napoli, Donna Jo.
The prince of the pond: otherwise known as De Fawg Pin / by Donna Jo Napoli;
illustrated by Judith Byron Schachner.—1st ed.   p.   cm.
Summary: Having been turned into a frog by a hag, a frog-prince makes
the best of his new life as he mates, raises a family, and
instills a new kind of thinking into his frog family.
ISBN 0-525-44976-0
[1. Frogs—Fiction.] I. Schachner, Judith Byron, ill. II. Title.
PZ7.N15Pr   1992   91-40340   [Fic]—dc20   CIP   AC

Puffin Books ISBN 0-14-037151-6

Printed in the United States of America

To our families,
near and far, up and down and sideways,
and to Lucia, with love.

DONNA JO AND JUDY

I thank Joanne Casullo, who opened
my eyes to the other sides of fairy tales
with her wonderful poem. May all our
frogs sit under gibbous moons.

D. J. N.

⟶ Table of Contents ⟵

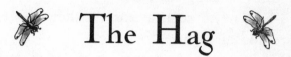

CHAPTER ONE

The Hag

He was sitting in the middle of the slate walk by the hag's house. I knew immediately I'd never seen him before.

"Hey," I called.

He looked at me with one eye. I waited for him to leap over beside me. He didn't move.

"Well, don't just sit there. Get off the walk."

He blinked. His skin looked strange. Almost dusty, like a toad's. But he was no toad.

"What's the matter with your mucus glands?" I said.

He twisted his upper body and thrust it forward, cocking his head.

I had never seen a frog do that before. "Are you all right?"

He blinked. He looked at me with one eye. Then he turned his head and looked with the other eye. His head jerked from side to side. It was as though he wanted to see me with both eyes at once. I couldn't imagine why.

"What's the matter with your eyes?" I said.

He sat very still.

Near him was a pile of cloth. Even from where I sat in the dirt under the scraggly rosebush I could make out dark blue shiny stuff and the soft rumples of deep yellow fuzzy stuff. In the middle was a cap made of animal skin with plumes sticking out of it. I'd been around enough to recognize what this stuff was: the clothes of a human. There was probably a naked human close by. "You better get over here before the human comes."

He jumped at that. But it wasn't an ordinary jump. It wasn't the high hop of a
toad or the long leap of a frog. His right
foreleg stuck straight out ahead. His left
flew up at an angle and smacked him
square in the face. His hind legs, which
were of extraordinary bulk and power, shot
out behind him and crossed each other. He
landed in a splat on his pale belly and
bounced.

I came out from under the bush, looking in every direction. "Are you still alive?"
I called.

His webbed feet were hooked together at the ankle. He bent his knees and straightened his legs and bent his knees and straightened his legs, but he couldn't get his feet unhooked.

I jumped closer.

His eyes were frantic. He thrashed around.

"You're making a spectacle of yourself," I said. "If the naked human doesn't get you, a hawk will."

He opened his mouth and his long tongue flopped out. He drew it back in with difficulty. "Hep," he said. "Hep, hep."

"Hep?" I jumped beside him. A bird swooped over the witch-hazel bush. It was a harmless swallow, thank heavens. "Hep?"

He rolled onto his back and threw his forelegs about.

"Stop it," I said. "What ridiculous behavior!" I flicked my tongue and lassoed his right ankle. I gave a strong tug. His feet came unhooked. A delicious-looking aphid scooted off the slate into the grass, heading straight for my rosebush. I leaped after it.

"Hep!" he called again.

I swallowed the aphid. Then I looked at the newcomer. He was still on his back.

"Hep," he said. "Hep me."

"Hep me?" I thought about it. "Hep me. Hmmmm. Oh, *help* me. You mean *help me.*"

He moved his head up and down vigorously. His tongue fell out of his mouth.

I jumped aside in case he was about to throw another fit.

He stopped moving and looked at me with an emotion I had never before seen in a frog's eyes. He didn't want to fight me or mate with me or scare me off. He wanted something I couldn't understand. His eyes bulged, the normal gold-colored irises bright and intelligent. But there was that mysterious something else.

I wasn't used to helping other frogs. But, then, I wasn't used to being asked to help, either. This was an unusual frog. Big, too. And good-looking. I jumped near and gave him a shove. He flipped over and sat with his short forelegs splayed. That's when I happened to glance up the walk. "The hag's coming! Hurry!" I leaped back under the rosebush.

"Hag," he said slowly.

"Hurry, you crazy frog!"

He looked up the walk. The hag had stopped at her herb garden. Several plants lay flat on the ground, crushed. She straightened one thistle plant carefully, crooning to herself and swaying from side to side. The crystal in her ring glowed amber.

The stranger looked back at me with desperate eyes. "How?" he said.

"What's the matter with you?" I shouted. "Hurry!"

And he did the second strangest jump I'd ever witnessed and landed splud, sploof, right in the thorn branches. "Yeeeeoooowww!"

"Oh me, oh me, oh me, oh me." I shook the branches till he fell on the dirt beside me. "This way. Little jumps. You hear me? L-i-t-t-l-e. No more big jumps. You got it?"

He threw his head up and down again the way he had done when he was on his back on the slate walk.

I took a little jump and disappeared into the grasses. "Come on," I whispered back to him.

He landed in front of me on his head.

I jumped forward and shoved him again. This time he righted himself quickly.

The hag was now beside the pile of clothes, searching through them. She picked up the plumed cap and flipped it onto her head while she cackled softly.

"Where are you, froggy? I've brought you a present." She held up a crippled cockroach and cackled again. "Your first meal as a frog. Doesn't it look scrumptious?" There was a wet whistling noise from her beaked nose. "Where are you?" She held up the blue shiny stuff. It was a

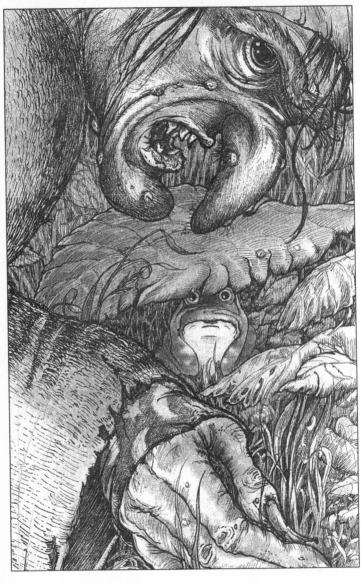

ruffled shirt. She shook it hard, then she threw it down.

"You thought you could just come marching along, looking so handsome and jaunty, didn't you?" She held up the yellow fuzzy stuff. It was a pair of trousers. She felt in the pockets. "I saw that smug look on your face." She ripped the trousers in half and threw them down.

She stood upright and scratched her skinny, knobby throat thoughtfully. "Crossing my land. Trampling my thistle patch." She gave a little shudder. "Poor thistle. Why, I can make the best choking potion ever from that marvelous thistle." She looked down at the pile of clothes. "No respect!" she screamed. "No respect at all!" Her eyes grew small, and her voice was like a thin reed. "I hate the sight of you! You and your whole royal family. All you big-footed, smiley-mouthed nincompoops. I hate you all!" She twisted her hands together and hissed like a snake. "But this time I got you!"

She kicked through the clothes with the sharp tips of her black boots. Then she looked up and down the slate path, in the grass on both sides, now under the rosebush where I'd been just a moment ago. She was curved over with her nose only inches from the ground, and I could see the black hairy growths on her teeth. I was grateful in that moment that frogs don't have a good sense of smell. The air that whistled in and out of her nose was wet and hot. My skin quivered.

Slowly she shook her head, and a thin smile made its way across her face. "Ha. I showed you, didn't I? No matter where you are now, you're not safe. Anyone and anything can hurt you. And no one will ever think you are handsome or jaunty again. Ha ha ha ha."

The hag did a crazy dance, pulling the plumes out of the hat as she twirled and swirled. "Maybe I'll even eat you someday, froggy. Maybe I'll catch you next time I fix a froggy stew for me and my bats." She laughed. "If you live that long!"

I sat motionless.

Fortunately, the big male did the same.

CHAPTER TWO

 Water

"You're certainly fat enough," I said, inspecting him all around. "You've been out of hibernation at least a month, I bet."

He sat in the damp hollow between the raised oak tree roots and breathed deeply. He blinked his eyes over and over again.

I had already recovered from our close scrape with the hag. After all, a frog spends life leaping out of the way of predators. But the stranger still seemed in a state of shock. I watched his chest rise and fall. "You're the biggest green frog I've ever seen."

He stopped blinking and stared at me.

"I'd think you were a bullfrog if the skin folds on your sides didn't go all the way down to your hind legs."

He opened his mouth and his tongue fell out.

"What's the matter with your tongue?" I said. "Snap it back inside quick."

He pulled his tongue back into his mouth awkwardly, as if he wasn't used to doing this dozens of times a day.

"That's better." I looked him over. "I'm sorry if I offended you. You're a handsome green frog. Nothing like those boorish, gluttonous bullfrogs. I like the black splotches on your back and sides. They're distinguished. And your throat is creamy yellow. Very nice."

"Fawg," he said.

"Fawg?" I thought that over. "Did you say *fawg?*"

"Fawg," he said.

"Well, I don't know what *fawg* means," I said. I noticed something move over on the other side of the oak root. "Sit still," I said.

"Am I a fawg?" he said louder.

"Are you a fawg? Oh, are you a *frog?*" I shut my mouth and waited. I'd never heard an adult frog ask such a question before. I mean, sure, tadpoles ask it all the time: Am I a frog yet? Am I a frog yet? But this fellow's body was almost twice as long as mine. His tadpole days were a distant memory. I spoke carefully. "Yes, you are a frog." I swallowed. "And a very fine one."

He hung his head. "I'm a fawg."

Suddenly someone hopped from the oak root onto the wet dirt right in front of us. It was a big, brown, bumpy toad. "Get out," he barked.

"Oh, now, you don't have to be so rude." I looked at the stranger, who sat quietly beside me. "Come on, let's go."

"Fawg," said the stranger to the toad.

"Fawg?" asked the toad.

"He means *frog*," I said.

"Frog?" said the toad. "I'm no frog!"

"Of course you're not," I said. "He means he's a frog."

"Well, I know that," said the toad. "Anyone can see he's a frog."

"Fawg," said the stranger again in a sad voice.

The toad hopped close to him. "Don't say *frog* again."

"Fawg," said the stranger.

The toad hopped right beside him. "I'll frog you all right."

"Leap," I shouted to the stranger. "Leap away. His skin is poison." I leaped out of the hollow into the grasses.

The stranger came catapulting after me.

He landed on his right shoulder with a thud. He quickly got back into normal crouching position.

"Don't play games with toads," I said.

"Toad?"

"Didn't you know that was a toad?" I

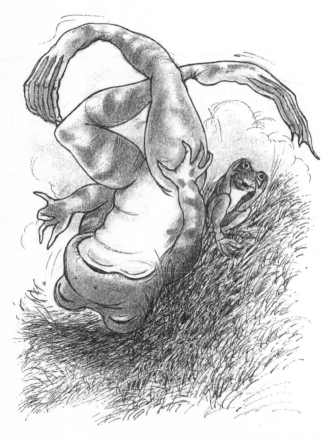

leaned away from the stranger. "Can't you tell a toad from a frog?"

He shook his head.

Now I leaned toward him. "Oh me, oh me, oh me, oh me. How on earth have you survived so long without knowing that?" I stared at him.

He didn't answer.

"Well, you certainly won't last very long around this pond if you don't learn fast," I said. I cleared my throat and spoke in my most commanding voice. "A toad has dry, warty skin." I looked hard at him. "A frog has wet, smooth skin. Got that?"

He blinked.

"A toad has bean-shaped bumps behind his eyes and sometimes even between his eyes and other places, too. A frog has, at most, lovely folds of skin here or there."

He blinked.

"A toad likes dark places and is gloomy. A frog enjoys the sun and is a happy sort." I leaped in a circle around him to make my point. "Understand?"

His face stayed sad. If I weren't so patient by nature, I might have left him right then. But he was so very unusual, who knew what he'd do next? I sat and stared at him, waiting.

He blinked. "Poy-en," he said.

"Poy-en?" I searched my brain. "Poy-en, poy-en. What on earth? Oh, poison? Is that what you said, poison?"

He blinked.

"Yes, most toads have toxins in their skin. Most frogs do, too. Even you, though your poison isn't strong enough to make anything really sick. But that toad's poison is strong. You'd die if you stayed in the hollow with him."

He looked properly impressed.

"Actually, some frogs and toads are hard to tell apart. But if he's short, fat, and ugly, with squat little legs, bet he's a toad and you'll probably be right." I listened to the growl of my stomach. "Let's go eat." I leaped off toward the pond.

The stranger jumped in his own peculiar way, staying pretty much by my side, making better and better jumps as he went.

The pond was close. I never stray too far from water. I'm a sensible sort. We sat on the mud at the edge. The soft wet squish was a delight to my sensitive skin. "Doesn't that feel just right?" I said.

"Mud," he said, lifting one foot, then another. "Muddy, muddy mud."

The mud was full of all kinds of yummy things. "Look!" In the flick of a tongue I ate a slug.

"Ugh," he said. He leaned over the water and jumped back as if in terror. Then he leaned over again and stared.

I stared, too. There was nothing there. Only the big male's reflection.

"Mmm," he said, shaking his head slowly. Then he put his mouth in the water.

"What on earth are you doing?" I pushed him.

He fell face first into the water. Then he coughed and jumped back onto the mud.

"No self-respecting amphibian drinks," I said. "We absorb water through our skin. If you're thirsty, take a swim."

"Wim," he said.

"Yes, swim." I leaped into the water. "Come on."

He jumped in beside me and thrashed

his forelegs like a paddle wheel. He kicked his hind legs out in front. He sank.

I lassoed him with my tongue and pulled him to shore. "Don't you even know how to swim?"

"I wim," he said.

"Oh no you don't," I said. "That was the poorest excuse for swimming I ever saw." I

leaped back into the water. "Watch. The power's in your hind legs, like this. See?"

He watched in silence.

"Come on, give it a try. I won't let you drown."

He jumped in and flailed a bit. But soon he was making smooth circles that shot him through the water at a decent frog speed.

"I'm a special green frog," I said, gliding along beside him. "The hag imported some of my ancestors from France a long time ago. When she comes frogging, she sings a little song about how delicious we are."

The stranger looked at me and paled a little. I was glad to see he knew to be afraid of the hag, at least. Even if he didn't know toads were dangerous, he knew the hag was.

"You can tell the special green frogs because we have two vocal sacs." I held my head up high out of the water so he could see. "One on each side of the head, instead of a single one on the throat."

The stranger swam around me in an oval.

I inspected his head as he swam past. "I see you've got two vocal sacs, too. But

you're a slightly different type of green frog, aren't you?" I said.

The stranger stopped and bobbed gently in the water beside me. "I'm a pin," he said.

"A pin." I flicked my tongue out and swallowed a snail.

"You can caw me Pin," said the stranger.

"I can *call* you Pin." I'd never known a frog with a name. But the stranger was different. He looked different, and he acted different. And if he wanted a name, it was okay with me. I sort of liked the idea. "Pin is a good name," I said. "Hello, Pin."

CHAPTER THREE

The Turtle

"What dat?" said Pin, leaping along the mud at the edge of the pond.

"That's a water sow bug," I said. "How can you ask what it is? Are you feeling all right?" I stared at him. "You know water sow bugs, Pin. You have to. You must have eaten hundreds of them in your life. Every pond frog has."

Pin swatted at the sow bug with his forefoot. It flew out of the shallow water onto the mud. I'd never seen a frog swat at something like that before. Pin stared at the seven pairs of thrashing legs on the turned-over sow bug. "Not bug," he said.

"Well, you're right. It's not a bug. It's a crustacean. But we call it a bug because it's so small."

"Tiny obteh," he said.

"Obteh?"

"Tiny cayfih," he said.

"Cayfih? Cayfih? Oh, *crayfish*. Yes. And *obteh* must be lobster. Yes." I looked at Pin with new interest. The water birds that stopped here every spring and fall talked sometimes about the sea creatures, and I had heard them describe lobsters. Most of the frogs I knew were too afraid of being eaten to do anything but dive underwater when the birds came. I didn't dive, though.

I hid among the rocks and listened. The other frogs knew only about the pond they lived in. But I knew whatever I overheard the birds say. I knew about the huge wonderful world away from this pond. Pin must be a curious frog, like me. "Yes, yes," I said, leaping closer to Pin. "The sow bug is like a tiny lobster."

The sow bug righted itself. Pin swatted it onto its back again. "Obteh good to eat," said Pin.

"Who are you kidding? You've never tasted a lobster," I said.

"I have eaten obteh," said Pin. "Many time."

"What a story!" I said. "Lobsters live in salt water. Amphibians don't. You've never been near a lobster." I shot out my tongue and ate the sow bug. "Don't give yourself airs. I'm impressed by your size alone. You don't need to make up silly stories about eating lobster."

"I have eaten obteh many time!" Pin drummed his forelegs in the mud. "Many time!"

At that moment the mud moved. I

leaped for the grassy bank. "Leap, you crazy frog," I shouted. "Leap, leap!"

Pin stayed in his crouch, and the mud lifted up right under him.

"Oh, leap!" I hopped about in the grass wildly. I feared the worst. And my fear was right: It was the dreaded snapping turtle! Pin sat smack-dab in the middle of the back of the most hideous creature of the pond.

What was the matter with that frog? He acted like he hadn't felt the movement in the mud, but all frogs feel the slightest movement, even in dry ground. Pin should have recognized the danger instantly. He should have leaped for safety, like any sensible frog. Like me.

Instead, he sat there, looking around. Helpless. It was as though he didn't know the first thing about pond life. Oh, poor dead frog. And just when it was beginning to get interesting knowing him.

The turtle shook the mud off its face and lifted its horny head high. "Who's that on my back?"

"Pin," said Pin.

"Pin? Who are you, Pin?"

"Fawg," said Pin.

"Fawg?" The turtle twisted its neck so that it could see Pin sitting on the high ridge of its shell. "You're a frog."

"De Fawg Pin," Pin said.

"De Fawg Pin?" The turtle snapped at the air a few times. "Well, come on down here where I can eat you."

"I'm not dumb," said Pin. His tongue fell out. He pulled it back in. I had to admit he looked dumb when he did that.

"Hmmm," said the turtle. "You're on my back. You're pretty dumb."

"No," said Pin. "You under me. You petty dumb."

"You talk funny," said the turtle.

Pin blinked.

"Okay, wise guy," said the turtle. "Just try to get off of me. I'll snap you in half."

"Bad idea," said Pin.

The turtle took a few steps forward. "Did you fall off yet?"

"You dumb," said Pin. "Dumb, dumb, dumb."

"You're making me mad," said the turtle.

32

"You mad? I'm de one mad," said Pin. "I'm a fawg."

"What are you saying?" said the turtle. "What does being a frog have to do with being mad?"

"I'm mad at being a fawg. Oh, am I mad," said Pin.

"You're mad at being a frog?" said the turtle.

"Mad," said Pin. "You one dumb tuh-tuh, and I'm one mad fawg."

"You're going to be one dead fawg in a minute," said the turtle. He leaned way to the left.

Pin slid to the left.

The turtle snapped just as Pin managed to pull himself back up to the ridge of the shell.

The turtle leaned way to the right.

Pin slid to the right.

The turtle snapped again, and again Pin managed to get back to the high ridge just in time.

"You de king of dumb," said Pin. "You can't get me."

"Yes I can," said the turtle. He leaned way to the right, but Pin leaped up and landed right on the shell ridge. He leaned way to the left, but Pin leaped again.

Right.

Leap.

Left.

Leap.

"All right," shouted the turtle. "This is

war." He leaned all the way to the right and flipped over just as Pin leaped onto the mud.

The turtle whipped around on its back and snapped. But Pin leaped again, into the tall grasses beside me. "Hi," he said.

I stared at him.

"I'll get you yet," shouted the turtle as he struggled to stick his saw-toothed tail down into the mud.

"You too dumb," Pin shouted back.

"You're the dumb one!"

"Den why you on back and I not in tummy?"

"Next time," screamed the turtle. His tail was now fully in the mud. He used it to flip himself back onto his feet. "Next time!"

Pin leaped back toward the turtle.

"Stop," I called after him. "Stay away from reptiles. He'll kill you."

Pin picked up a stick in his mouth. I'd never seen a frog with a stick in his mouth before. My jaw fell open, and my tongue lolled out. Right then I must have looked like him when his tongue fell out. I snapped

my tongue back in my mouth. Pin looked at the turtle and spit the stick through the air.

The turtle snapped the stick in half.

Pin picked up a rock in his mouth and looked at me.

"You're very crazy," I said.

Pin spit the rock at the turtle.

The turtle snapped at the rock. "Owwwww!" he screamed. "That hurt!"

Pin leaped back beside me. "Dumb, dumb, dumb," he said.

CHAPTER FOUR

Food

"You can't sit on a lily pad all day long in the hot sun without eating." I snapped a dragonfly out of the air and let it fall on the lily pad in front of Pin. "You've gone three whole days with no food. It's not right. It's not froglike."

Pin kicked the dragonfly into the water.

"You're one stubborn frog, you know that?" A small painted turtle swam by and snapped up the dragonfly. "What a waste," I said. "Listen, Pin, you told the snapping turtle you were mad. You told the wood frog you were mad. You even told the stupid caecilian, that's hardly better than a worm, that you were mad. But I simply don't understand. What are you so mad about?"

"I can't expain," said Pin.

"Expain! It's not *expain*, it's *explain*."

"I can't expain," said Pin.

"Try."

Pin looked at me. Then he looked out across the pond. Then he looked up toward the sky. Then he looked at me again. "I mih my wohd."

I didn't understand. "Try again."

He shook his head in frustration. "I'm new to de pond. I don't have…" He sighed. "I don't have my home." His eyes were big and sad. "I'm not me. I'm no one. I can't even tawk."

I thought about that. Pin was certainly someone. He was a big green frog. But it was true, he had a lot of trouble talking. "You know, I've got it figured out. You can't say *llll*, can you?"

Pin didn't answer.

"And you can't say *shhhh* either. Or *rrrr* or *zzzz* or *ssss* or *thhhh*. That's why you say *obteh* for *lobster* and *poy-en* for *poison* and *dat* for *that*."

Pin looked at me in silence.

"What's your problem?" I asked. "Why can't you talk right?"

"My tongue," said Pin.

"Your tongue? Stick out your tongue."

Pin opened his mouth, and his tongue lolled out.

"You have a perfectly normal tongue."

Pin pulled his tongue back in his mouth. "My tongue attached at bad point. It faw out."

"Your tongue is attached at the front of your mouth, just like all frogs' tongues."

Pin stamped his forelegs. "My tongue new. It too ong. Too ong and too fat."

I looked at him. "All frogs' tongues are long and fat."

Pin blinked. "I hate my new tongue. I can't move it ight."

His new tongue. Why did he keep saying such strange things? And what a complainer Pin was turning out to be. As though moving his tongue was some sort of difficult task! I saw a ripple in the water off to our left. I sat very still. No more ripples. It was probably just bird droppings, thank heavens. I looked at Pin and shook my head and sighed. "You can't talk and you're mad and you act loopy."

"Oopy?" said Pin.

"Loopy. Like you didn't know the first thing about toads. And then you didn't recognize that the snapping turtle was under you. And I had to give you that whole big long lesson about danger: about raccoons and turtles and water birds and bullfrogs and especially snakes." I shivered at the very thought of water snakes. "There's something wrong, Pin."

Pin looked at me. "I tode you. I'm not me. I can't expain any betteh." He hung his head.

"That's enough! No more glum faces around here!" I dove into the water and came up with a glass worm. I plopped it on the lily pad. "Eat, Pin. Happy or sad, eat! That's an order."

He kicked the glass worm into the water.

"All right, that's it. You don't like insects. You don't like worms. What on earth do you eat? Besides lobster, that is."

"Meat."

"Meat? Like baby mice? Don't tell me you eat small mammals like a bullfrog does."

"No. Big animow. Beef."

"Beef?" I'd never heard of it. "What is beef?"

"Meat of cow," said Pin.

"Cow? You mean those big land animals that eat grass on the other side of the pond?"

Pin nodded. "Cow. My cow. Dey my cow." His voice was mournful. "Dey my cow, and I eat cow."

"They're your cows, and you eat cows," I said slowly.

Pin blinked.

No, it couldn't be. I looked hard at his jawline. "Open your mouth."

He opened his mouth. His tongue fell out. He quickly snapped it back in. Thank heavens he was doing better with his tongue, at least.

I inspected carefully. "Okay, shut it."

He shut his mouth.

"You're a liar," I said.

"Huh?"

"You have the same mouth I do. Your jaw is wide, but it isn't hinged like a snake's. You can't swallow anything that's bigger than the rim of your mouth. You can't eat a cow!"

"I eat cow," said Pin. "I bite."

"Oh, I see you have some little teeth there. But don't think that shocks me. I've known frogs with teeth before. The wood frog has a row of sharp teeth, too. But hers are tiny, and so are yours. They're too tiny to do anything but hold your prey in place while you prepare to swallow it. They can't rip anything. They can't chew."

Pin blinked.

I felt sorry for him. "Listen, even if you tried to eat a cow, it would only step on you and squash you."

"I eat dead cow."

"*Dead* cow? A frog never eats anything that doesn't move." I saw something dart through the water. I dove and came up with a minnow. I threw it on the lily pad, and it flopped around.

Pin looked at it.

"Fish is like meat," I said.

"Dead," he said.

"It'll be dead in a minute," I said. "Just wait."

When the fish stopped moving, Pin flicked his tongue out and touched it lightly. "Ugh."

"Don't be picky."

He blinked, and with a flick of the tongue the minnow disappeared into his mouth.

"See?" I said.

An instant later he spit out the minnow.

"You're ridiculous. This is your last chance." I leaned over the lily pad. "Look, there goes another. Go for it."

Pin dove into the water. He came up with a small crayfish hanging on to his bottom jaw. "Hep me," he shouted. "Hep me."

I pulled the crayfish off and put it on Pin's lily pad. "Come eat it."

He shook his head.

"Come on," I said. "It's just like a baby lobster."

Pin shook his head again. "Too haad," he said. "Too haad to eat." He pushed his tongue against the crayfish's hard outer shell.

The crayfish grabbed onto Pin's tongue with one claw.

"Aaaaa!" screamed Pin.

I knocked the crayfish off. "Your stom-

ach acids will dissolve his hard shell. You can even eat small turtles if you want. Now there's good meat, they say, turtle meat. The bullfrogs eat them all the time. And I would rejoice to see you eat a turtle, after all the green frogs I've seen get eaten by turtles." I watched the juicy crayfish with growing hunger. "Come on, eat the crayfish."

Pin swam in a circle, eyeing the crayfish on the lily pad.

The crayfish held up its claws and threatened.

"Pin, be brave. You're not a tiny spring peeper. You're a giant for a green frog. And this is a small crayfish. Eat him!"

Pin circled the lily pad again. Then he jumped up on my lily pad beside me. "Cook," he said.

"Cook? You want to cook the crayfish?"

Pin blinked.

The crayfish flipped itself into the water and disappeared.

"Pin, frogs don't cook their food."

Pin lifted his chin toward the sun.

"You look like a statue of the perfect

frog," I said. "But you're half-starved, and if you insist on cooked crayfish, you're going to be fully starved very soon."

"Dead," said Pin.

"That's what they call it," I said. "Dead. You talk about being no one. Well, dead is being no one." I felt the breeze cool my wet skin and make it quiver. "Oh me, oh me, oh me, oh me. If you starve, Pin, there are so many froggy happy days that you'll never know."

"Happy day?" said Pin.

"Yes, of course. Frogs are always happy. I told you that. We're not melancholy like toads."

"Happy fawg," said Pin, without conviction. "Dead may be betteh."

"How can you think that? Staying alive is what it's all about. I don't understand you one bit." I looked at his fine green body and thought of how I was getting used to his funny way of talking. I sighed. "If you starve, I'll be all alone again."

Pin looked at me. "You want me wid you?"

I thought about how odd he was. About all his unfroglike ways. I had stayed with him against my better judgment. I couldn't help myself. Pin was crazy. An utterly mad frog. But he was new and interesting and even fun. "Yes," I said, half-surprised at my own words. "I want you with me."

Pin took a deep breath. Suddenly there was a gleam in his eye that hadn't been there before. He snapped himself to attention. In an instant he flicked out his tongue and swallowed a gnat.

I leaned toward him. "How was it?"

"Not bad."

We sat in silence, motionless.

A moment later he flicked out his tongue and swallowed a mosquito.

"You fine big frog," I said.

Pin leaped onto his own lily pad. He landed in a crouch, just like any other frog.

CHAPTER FIVE

Singing

Pin sat on a rock in the early evening. I leaped over and landed so that my hind leg was lightly brushing the rock. It was still warm from the day's sun. Pin looked at me with interest. I was delighted to see that his eyes were finally coordinated—no more of that one-eye-then-the-other-eye-then-the-first-eye business. His skin glistened, even though he hadn't been in the water for at least an hour. He had learned how to use his mucus glands. He had learned how to take advantage of his flexible joints in leaping, too. And he could sense movement in the water or on the mud with his feet and skin just as well as I could.

I had taught him all of that, slowly, day by day. I'd been astonished at what he didn't know. Things that came naturally to other frogs Pin had to learn in little steps. At first it was as though he didn't even know how his own body worked. But he was a fast learner. I didn't know how he had managed to stay alive before he met me. He never answered when I asked that. But however he had managed, I was glad he had. He didn't complain anymore. And his tongue hardly ever fell out of his mouth these days. "You are the finest frog," I said.

A spotted newt slithered through the algae at the edge of the pond. It was olive green with red and black spots on its back.

"Petty newt," said Pin.

"Pretty?" I'd never thought of newts that way.

From way off in the reeds a bullfrog came flying at the newt. But the newt disappeared into the muddy bank in the nick of time.

The bullfrog got a mouth full of mud. He splashed back into the pond.

I gulped. "Dirty bullfrog! If we were froglets, we'd be in mortal danger now. I think we'd better move anyway, in case he gets the idea of attacking us."

"Nuh-uh," said Pin. "No buhfawg attack Pin."

"Now, Pin, don't get me started on that

again. I've told you a dozen times: The pond is full of danger. And we have no defenses. Anybody big enough and fast enough can eat us."

"Don't tawk," said Pin. He looked out over the water.

I hushed up and looked, too. The bullfrog's eyes peeked up out of the water and stared straight at us. I tightened up for a leap. Then the bullfrog suddenly swam away in the other direction. "Well, it looks like you're right this time," I said.

"Tiny buhfawg," said Pin.

"Well, I guess he wasn't that big," I said. "But did you see how far he leaped at that newt? That was far even for a bullfrog. Green frogs leap only about seven or eight times their body length at most. I bet even you can't leap much more than that. But the bullfrog did."

Pin looked at his hind legs. Then he looked back at me.

"We'd better stay alert," I said.

It was the first of June, and Pin and I had been together for more than a month. The flatworms in the pond had given way to the aquatic insects. The mites swam about rapidly like tiny bright red spiders. The water fleas swarmed all over each other in delicious profusion. The stupid little cyclops bumped around the shallows blindly with their antennae flopping. Pin's tongue shot out and a cyclops disappeared. Oh, what a fine frog he was.

"What dat?" said Pin.

I looked. What I saw made me turn pale. "Water scorpions," I said.

"Aaaaa," said Pin. "Dey bad?"

I looked at the small insects. There were dozens of them. And more were to follow, I knew that only too well. "They come to eat the water fleas, but they stick around to eat the tadpoles. They're even more dangerous to tadpoles than the dragonfly larvae that lurk on the bottom of the pond."

"No tadpoe yet," said Pin.

"No, but it's time very soon," I said. I leaped up onto the rock beside him. "Soon the waters will be filled with eggs." I let my foreleg touch his. "Soon."

Pin looked at me with uncertainty in his eyes.

I looked across the pond. The evening chorus of frogs had begun. "Do you like singing?" I asked.

"Yup," said Pin. These days he had taken to saying *yup* instead of blinking.

We sat motionless for a few minutes. "The frogs sing every night," I said.

"Why?" said Pin.

"Why do they sing? Well, because it's that time of year."

"What time of ye-ah?"

"When frogs mate," I said. The spotted newt peeked his head out of the mud bank. "See that newt?" I said. "He's got a hard job. He's going to have to parade around a female and curl up his tail facing her and release his stinky little scent and use

his waving tail to make the fumes go her way. Then if he's lucky, she'll let him mate. I love to watch the ritual. It's unfroglike, but very interesting."

I pressed my foreleg gently against Pin's. "That's what the newt has to do. But all a frog has to do is sing. We're very lucky for amphibians. It's a simple courtship." I looked at him in silence.

Pin kept his eyes on the newt.

"Would you like to sing?" I asked softly.

"Me? Ing?" Pin took a deep breath. Then he spoke slowly, with a slight tremble in his voice. "At home I ang often." He looked at me. "Now I can't even tawk ight. How could I ing?"

I was baffled for a moment. Then I realized how confused Pin was. "Oh, Pin. Singing is nothing like talking! You don't have to use your tongue to sing."

Pin looked away. Finally, he looked back at me. "How?"

"Use your sacs, of course."

Pin looked alarmed.

I nudged the tip of my face up against

the sac on the side of his head. "These sacs. Your vocal sacs."

Pin moved to the edge of the rock and leaned over the side.

"What are you doing?"

"I'm ooking," said Pin. "I'm ooking in wateh."

I made a small jump and landed beside him. I leaned over to see what he was looking at. "Oh, you want to see your reflection in the water. Well, there's one sac," I said, nudging him on his right vocal sac. I leaped across him. "And there's the other," I said, nudging him on the other vocal sac.

"Hmmm," said Pin. He sat silent for another minute. Then he said, "How?"

"Well"—I hesitated—"well, I don't really know."

Pin looked at me.

"I mean, I guess you just sort of have to want to sing. I mean, how could I know? I'm a female, and in my family only the males are musicians."

Pin stared out across the water.

"Look, you're a resourceful frog," I said. "Experiment."

Pin blinked his eyes rapidly. His body trembled. His skin turned a brownish green. Then he looked at me. "I have no ong."

"Any song will do," I said. "Just swallow air and start. I mean, when most frogs do it, they swell up their sacs like little balloon bubbles."

Pin opened his mouth and snapped it shut. Then he burped. He opened his mouth again and snapped it shut again. He burped again.

I was embarrassed for him. "Maybe I'll take a swim," I said. I dove into the water and swam a good twelve feet in the opposite direction the bullfrog had gone. Then I let myself hang suspended on the surface of the water, just drifting along. The tip of my mouth and both nostrils and both eyes stuck up out of the water. The rest of me floated below, brushed softly by the waterweeds. I felt dreamy, as though there was nothing in this pond except me and Pin. Pin, my big, handsome, wonderful frog.

I watched him the whole time. He kept doing the oddest things. He stretched his legs out and curled the four fingers on each forefoot and the five toes on each hind foot. He hopped in place. He flipped over and landed on his back but managed to get upright again in a flash. I could hear his sigh of despair. I drifted closer.

All of a sudden he jumped up and down and flailed his forelegs. He hadn't had one of his fits since the very first day I'd met him. But it looked like he was having another at this very moment. "Nake!" he shouted. "Nake, nake!"

Oh me. What could that poor twisted frog be trying to say? I swam toward him. I was about seven feet away now.

"Nake!" he shouted again. He turned pale and bounced up and down. "Nake, nake, nake!" He looked like he might bounce right off the rock and into the water. And in the crazy state he was in, he just might drown! I swam faster.

But suddenly Pin leaped that huge, long distance through the air, right toward me. I ducked and Pin landed with a whump, smack-dab on a water snake's head right beside me.

I swam for my life to the rock and

leaped from there to the safety of the bank. I was almost white with fright.

Pin landed beside me, bounced a few times, and came to a rest.

"You're crazy," I said. "You went the wrong way. You leaped right at the snake."

"Yup," said Pin.

"Snakes are our enemies, Pin. I told you before: Stay away from reptiles. I told you! Water snakes are the most horrible of all the reptiles! Oh, you never listen to me. You're as disobedient as a froglet. Worse, you acted like a tadpole. Whatever possessed you to leap at him?"

"You," said Pin.

"Me?"

"Nake about to eat you. I jump on nake. You not eaten."

"You jumped on the snake to stop him from eating me?"

"Yup."

"You jumped on the snake to save me?"

"Yup."

"That's the craziest idea I ever heard," I said.

Pin blinked.

I sat for several minutes thinking this over. "You saved me," I said at last. I leaped beside him. "You could have gotten eaten."

"I'm too big," he said.

"Well, I don't know about that." I thought about the water snake. It was a medium-sized one. "Sure, he could have swallowed me whole, and he couldn't have done that to you." I looked at Pin's huge body. "Still, he might have taken your leg off." I looked at Pin's legs. They were strong and glorious. "He could have eaten you bit by bit."

"He didn't," said Pin.

"Well, that's because he was so surprised," I said. "No sane frog would jump on a water snake's head. You're just lucky he was stunned." I looked back at the pond and thought some more. "You saved me," I said slowly. "That is a very crazy thing you did, but somehow it makes me happy."

"Don't tawk," said Pin. He sat very still, and his eyes shone like diamonds in the moonlight. His left vocal sac inflated. "Croak," he sang with half a voice.

"Yes," I whispered. "That's it."

He strained for a moment. His right vocal sac quivered, but no sound came. "Ight not ing," he said. "I can't. Oh, I can't do it."

"That's okay," I said. "Your voice is beautiful with only one vocal sac anyway."

Pin took a big breath. "Croak," he sang, his left vocal sac inflating and deflating over and over again. "Croak, croak, croak."

CHAPTER SIX

Eggs

"It's June fifth," I said.

Pin croaked with his left vocal sac.

"Do you know what tomorrow is?" I said.

Pin croaked with his left vocal sac.

"It's June sixth," I said. "Time is pass-
ing, Pin."

"Croak," he said.

I looked across the water around our lily
pad. There were small jelly-coated eggs all
through the aquatic weeds, floating on the
surface of the water. I eyed the loopy long

strings of toad eggs and the lovely black masses of frog eggs. There were thousands of them. But not a single one of those eggs was ours. "Pin, it's time for reproduction."

"No," said Pin.

"But why?"

"I tode you," said Pin.

"You'll have to tell me again," I said. "It's nonsense to worry about the water scorpions."

"Wateh copion eat tadpoe."

"So what if water scorpions eat tadpoles? I'll lay hundreds of eggs. Maybe even thousands. If the water scorpions eat most of them, who cares?"

"I do."

As if to make Pin's point, a water scorpion flew down into the reeds near us and scooped up a mouthful of frog eggs. He moved slowly and clumsily up a reed and clung there, digesting.

"Pin, come on," I said. "This attitude is not froglike. Frogs lay eggs. Then they leave. Insects come. Snakes and toads and bullfrogs come. Everything eats the eggs. And everything eats the tadpoles. It doesn't matter what happens to them. They're on their own."

"Not mine."

"Pin!" I lassoed my tongue around his right foreleg and held it up for him to see. "Take a look at your foot."

Pin looked at his foot.

"That black hairy pad on your palm and thumb, know what it's for?"

Pin stared at me.

"You developed that just for mating. That's what will allow you to hold me tight."

"Hode tight?" said Pin.

"Yes. You jump on my back and squeeze the eggs out."

"If I jump on you, you die," said Pin.

"Well..." I looked him up and down. "You might be right. Usually a male green frog is smaller than a female, so he doesn't hurt her when he climbs on top. But you're much bigger than I am."

"I'm big," said Pin. "I'm De Fawg Pin."

"I know. That's what I just said." I stretched my hind toes apart till the webbing between them was thin and translucent. "Here's what. You can pick me up instead."

"I pick you up?"

"Sure. You can hold me for a few hours. Or a day. Maybe two at most."

"Two day?"

"Well, all right, maybe even three."

Pin zapped a dragonfly out of the air and tossed it to me. I swallowed it with a blink. He seemed to be thinking. Then he said softly, "Tadpoe, what dey eat?"

"Algae, of course. Don't you remember scraping the algae off the bottom of things when you were little?"

"No big food? No big pant?"

"No, no big plants. All they eat is algae." I looked at him. "It's not our job to feed them, if that's what you're thinking. I told you, they take care of themselves. We just mate. Then we leave them."

"No," said Pin. He raised his froggy face into the wind. Then he leaped off the lily pad and swam to the far side of the pond.

My heart sank.

He leaped onto the muddy bank.

I could hardly stand to watch.

"Come," he shouted as he disappeared with one huge leap into the grass.

I followed quickly, searching through the grasses for my lovely big frog.

He was waiting for me in the rye. "Croak," he said with his left vocal sac.

"Where are we going?" I asked.

Pin leaped ahead, with me close behind. At first I thought he was heading back toward the hag's house, but then he veered to the north.

We traveled for the rest of the afternoon, till we came to a small pond. Pin leaped into the water.

I splashed in beside him. "Here?" I said, looking around in dismay.

"No," said Pin.

"Oh, good," I said. "This is a temporary pond. See? There are no fish. It will dry up before the tadpoles have a chance to metamorphose."

"Metamo..."

"Metamorphose," I said. "Change into frogs."

"Oh." Pin splashed about and ate three slugs.

"Where are we going?" I asked.

"Tomo-wow," he said. "Tomo-wow you know."

"Okay. I can wait until tomorrow to know." I rested beside him on a rock.

A grass frog croaked weakly at us from the bank. "Hey, strangers," he called.

"What is it?" I called back.

"That's the biggest green frog I've ever seen," he said.

"He's the biggest there is," I called back.

"Is that the giant green frog named Pin?" said the grass frog.

"Yes," I said.

Pin shot out his tongue and zapped a

mite. He lifted his chin. I could tell he was pleased the grass frog had heard of him.

"Is that the one that broke the tip off the snapping turtle's jaw in the southwest pond?" he said.

"Rumors, rumors," I said. "The turtle's jaw didn't break, it only got hurt."

"Is that the one that stunned the water snake?"

"The very same," I said.

"I'm De Fawg Pin," said Pin. And for the first time since I'd met him, he seemed

to radiate the true happiness of a frog.

"I knew it," said the grass frog. "I've got to go spread the word." He leaped off.

Pretty soon there were not just grass frogs but tree frogs and wood frogs and green frogs and even bullfrogs gathered in the weeds and on the lily pads and on the mud all around us in every direction. We slept, surrounded by their bulging eyes and enveloped in their nocturnal croaking.

In the morning Pin woke me with a splash. We ate our fill of water fleas and took off leaping across a meadow.

A brook burbled in the woods beyond. Pin went right for the brook and hopped along its edge till he reached a bridge. He leaped to the center of the bridge and sat there.

I leaped beside him. "Here?" I said, feeling totally confused. There was no pond in sight.

"No," said Pin.

"Good," I said. I waited for Pin to move on. But Pin didn't move. "What's the matter?"

"Many fih here," said Pin.

I looked in the brook. "Yes, I suppose there are many fish here."

"I came here when I young," said Pin.

"This is very far from our pond," I said doubtfully.

"Yup. Home fah away." Pin talked slowly, as if he were half dreaming. "I came here on ong tip."

I worked to figure that one out. "Oh, you came here on a *long trip*. Well, I'll say. Most frogs never travel this far."

"I caught fih here wid my fadeh."

"You caught *fish* here with your *father?*" I looked at Pin. It had been a long time since he'd last told me one of those crazy lies. "Listen, Pin, for one thing, frogs never go in fast waters like this. We only go in calm waters."

"I didn't go in wateh," Pin said. "My fadeh made good poe. I caught fih wid poe."

I stared at Pin. Where did these wild stories come from? I had seen humans catch fish with poles, but frogs would never think of such a thing. "Pin," I said gently, "frogs don't use fishing poles. And they never know their fathers." I sat silent a moment. Then I added, "Or their mothers."

Pin looked down at the brook. "I knew my fadeh. My fadeh good. My mudeh good." Pin stared at the water with a longing I couldn't understand. I stared down with him.

We sat that way for a long time. Then Pin leaped to the other side of the bridge and headed off through the woods.

Soon I could hear the familiar noises of a large pond. We came closer and closer. But then Pin passed right by the giant pond and traveled another half hour before he stopped.

I looked around. We were in a garden behind a place where humans lived. It was like the big human home back near our old pond—the one the hag called a palace. There was no water in sight. "Here?" I said with disbelief.

"Yup."

"You passed by that wonderful pond to bring me here?"

"Yup."

Pin leaped along a path through rose-bushes, took a big jump, and stopped abruptly on top of something. He sat there looking around.

"What are you doing?" I said.

"Come."

I leaped up beside him and looked around. We were sitting on a black thing with four legs and a straight back. It was made of metal that felt nicely warm in the sun.

"I came here ong ago. I knew human here. I payd here."

"You *played* here." I sighed. "Pin…"

Then I shut my mouth. There was no use in arguing if he was going to persist in these lies. Besides, he looked sad again. Like he looked when he sat on the bridge over the brook. I didn't want him to be sad.

"In de pa-ah many human."

"In the *palace* are many humans. Yes," I said.

"Dey tawk and eat and have fun. Dey not fawg."

I didn't know what to say. Of course the humans weren't frogs. I looked around hoping to see a pond but knowing full well there was none near. Oh dear. "Pin," I said, "where's the water?"

"Behind dat hedge," said Pin. "We go behind dat hedge." He leaped off the black thing and around a hedge and jumped up onto a curved stone wall.

I jumped down onto the grass and leaped along the base of the wall. I moved close to the stones. They were cool and damp. There was water inside that circle of wall. Oh, joyous day. I jumped up onto the wall behind Pin. My momentary joy disappeared. "It looks deep," I said.

"No wateh copion," he said. "No wateh nake. No buhfawg."

"Well, okay, there are no water scorpions or water snakes or bullfrogs, but how will the new froglets get out when they're ready to move to land?"

"Dey can hop," said Pin.

"A froglet can't hop that far."

"Hmmm," said Pin. "Dey can hop on me."

"On your back?" I pictured it. "I like the idea. It's very amphibian of you."

Pin glowed. Then he dove in.

I did the same.

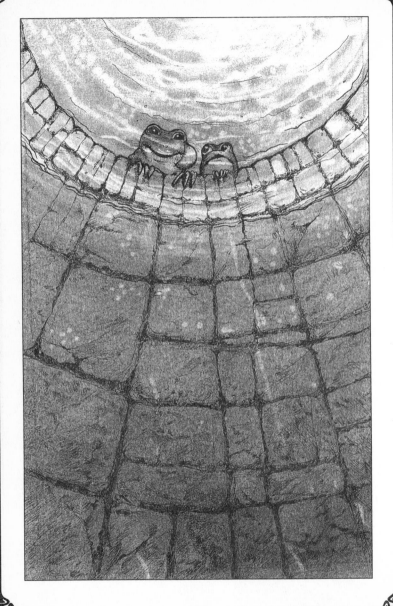

CHAPTER SEVEN

Tadpoles

Pin sat on the wall of our mating hole, as I had come to call this circle of water surrounded by stone, and stared into the water below.

"Any yet?" I called from the grass.

"No." He sighed. "No tadpoe."

"Don't worry," I said. "They'll hatch soon."

"No tadpoe," he said again.

"Listen, didn't you worry when the eggs sank, and didn't they come floating right back up to the surface like I promised? Just wait, they'll hatch today. I spawned them six days ago. You fertilized them immediately. They'll hatch today. I promise."

"Ook!" he shouted. "Ook, ook, ook!"

I leaped up onto the stone wall. "Look at them all. They're hatching by the dozens all at once."

"Dey wim!" said Pin.

"Of course they swim," I said. "They're tadpoles."

Within a few hours our mating hole was teeming with minute tadpoles. They flopped on top of one another. There were so many, the water looked dark brown and muddy.

"Why, they're going to smother each other," I said.

"What?" said Pin.

"There are too many of them for this small space. Oh me, oh me, oh me, oh me," I said. "There's not enough water, not enough room, not enough plant life in our mating hole to keep all those tadpoles alive. We've doomed them!"

Pin looked at me. His bright eyes were frantic. Then he dove right down into the mass of tadpoles. A moment later he leaped out with his mouth bulging. A tadpole slipped out. Pin kicked it back into the mating hole. Then he leaped off the wall, crossed the garden, and disappeared into the grasses beyond.

I waited on our mating hole wall a long

time, fretting over this turn of events. I hadn't known really what to expect. After all, Pin wasn't your normal frog. But for him to suddenly change into a tadpole-eating monster was a shock. Green frogs are not cannibals as a rule. Finally, I looked down into the swarm of pollywogs. One of them shouted up, "Am I a frog yet?" Tadpoles can be very stupid.

At that moment, Pin returned. "Time to dive," he said.

"Aren't you full yet?" I said.

Pin made the strangest noise I'd ever heard. Sort of a half croak, half gag. "I didn't eat dem," he said. "I bought dem to de pond." He made that noise again. "You funny," he said.

I stared at him. "What a brilliant frog you are! Sometimes you seem to know nothing and other times you know everything."

Pin dove into our mating hole. I dove after him. We filled our mouths and leaped back to the giant beautiful pond that was a half hour away. We worked all night long and all the next day. When there were only fifty tadpoles left in our mating hole, Pin stopped. "Dey tay," he said.

"They stay? Well, all right. I guess they'll be fine. There's plenty of room now, and plenty of food and oxygen."

"Am I a frog yet?" called up one of the tadpoles.

"Of course not, stupid," I called back.

"Tadpoe not tupid," said Pin.

Tadpoles *are* stupid, I thought. But I decided to let Pin learn that for himself.

We spent that night back at the giant pond on a granite rock near the center of the water.

"Don't you wish we'd come here in the first place?" I said.

"No," said Pin.

"But look at all that work we went through for nothing," I said. "Carrying all those tadpoles."

"Ook," said Pin. "Find tadpoe."

"That's easy," I said. "There's a tadpole there." A bullfrog swam by right then and swallowed the tadpole. "Well, there's another over there," I said. "There are dozens over there."

"My tadpoe?" asked Pin.

"Well, I don't know if they're yours," I said. "They're just tadpoles. Any frog's."

"Any toad," said Pin.

"Yes, or any toad's. So what's your point?"

"In de mating hoe, my tadpoe get big," said Pin.

I thought about that. "Not just your tadpoles; mine, too. Ours."

"I can't day *owww*," said Pin.

"You can't say *ours?* Oh, all right. So our tadpoles in our mating hole will grow big. They will survive. Yes, you're right."

"We have fifty tadpoe."

"Many more than that," I said.

A young water snake slid through the water with its mouth open and swallowed a few dozen tadpoles. It looked at us greedily.

"This is Pin," I shouted. "Famous Pin. De Fawg Pin."

The snake's eyes grew wide. He dove under the water and swam away.

"Well," I said, looking at the reduced group of tadpoles, "I guess maybe we can't count the ones in the pond here. Okay, we have fifty tadpoles that will make it for sure—all the tadpoles in our mating hole." I thought about our tadpoles in the mating hole, swimming around and playing diving games, perfectly safe and happy because of Pin. "That's good."

"Come," said Pin. "Feed tadpoe." Pin leaped out of the pond and across the grasses and back to the wall of our mating hole. He sat on the edge, motionless. I sat beside him. Within a few seconds a mosquito zipped by. Pin shot out his tongue. Then he dropped the mosquito into the mating hole.

"Yummy," screamed the tadpoles. "More, more, more."

"Don't jump on top of each other," I called down. "Take turns."

Pin dropped in a gnat. The tadpoles jumped on top of each other to get at it. Tadpoles are notoriously disobedient. So are froglets. That's why big frogs don't bother to try to teach them anything.

We sat there feeding them for hours. It was a bizarre thing to do—feeding tadpoles. But Pin was determined. It seemed to make him happy. And I didn't mind. For the next two months we came every day and dropped insects into the water. I was grateful we weren't common green frogs. Their tadpoles take a whole year to mature. Ours mature in a summer. I don't think I could have stood bringing the tadpoles insects every day for a year.

"Ook, ook," shouted Pin with glee at every new development. "Dey have bud." That's what he said when the tadpoles' hind leg buds appeared.

"Ook, ook," shouted Pin. "Dey have hind eg." That's what he said when the tadpoles' hind legs grew out of the buds.

"Ook, ook," shouted Pin. "Dey have bud again." That was when the tadpoles' foreleg buds appeared.

And, "Ook, ook," shouted Pin. "Dey have fo-we eg." That was when the tadpoles' fore-legs grew out of the buds.

"Ook, ook. No tay, no tay." That was when the tadpoles' tails started to shrink away. Pin hopped around me, shouting and chortling.

I didn't really understand why each change delighted him so. His antics were silly. But sweet silly. I found myself caught up in his excitement. We celebrated the meta-morphosis of our offspring together. I had to admit it was fun.

Finally, one late August day Pin shouted, "Ook, ook. Fawg!"

"Am I a frog yet?" shouted up a voice from our mating hole.

"Yup," shouted Pin. "You fawg."

"Fawg?" said the little voice. "I'm a fawg?"

"What about me?" called another voice.

"You fawg, too," said Pin.

"And me?" called another.

"Fawg," said Pin.

"We're all fawgs," shouted a fourth little voice. "Hurrah!"

Then Pin and I dove into the water and began the arduous job of carrying the heavy dear little froglets on our backs out of our mating hole. It took five trips to get them all safely to the pond.

CHAPTER EIGHT

Jimmy

Pin and I sat on our granite rock in the middle of the pond in the full sun. Jimmy sat between us.

Of the fifty froglets from our mating hole, Jimmy was the only one that had decided to stay with us. The others had quickly swum away in delight as soon as they reached the great freedom and excitement of this big pond. But Jimmy was different.

Pin had named him in an elaborate ceremony. He had danced around him and flipped over several times. Then he said, "I caw you Jimmy, afteh my fadeh."

Jimmy just nodded happily. He didn't think there was anything strange in a frog naming his froglet after his father. But, then, that's how froglets are—dumb and happy.

Then Pin looked over at me. "I caw you Jade."

I was taken aback. "Jade?"

"Yup. You Jade," said Pin. "You named Jade."

Pin was naming me. Jade. It was my name. A real name. He was the frog Pin and I was the frog Jade. I was special. At least, I was special to Pin. And I realized suddenly that Pin was special to me, too. I'd never met another frog I wanted to be with as much as Pin. I knew I never would again. He was my Pin. And I was his Jade. It was an amazing thing, this togetherness that Pin and I had. Amazing and wonderful.

I sat quietly under his gaze. I felt perfectly content.

Pin hopped close.

"I never heard the word *jade* before," I said.

"Jade a gem," said Pin. "A beautifuh gween gem. And you de moh beautifuh gween in de wohd. You gween ike jade."

"I'm the most beautiful green in the world," I whispered. "I'm green like jade." I looked at my reflection in his shining eyes.

"Yup," said Pin. "You my Jade."

Hearing Pin say my very thought made me happy. Oh, of course, I was always happy. I'm a frog, after all. But in that moment I felt I could burst from happiness. Rapture filled my heart. That was a foolish day. A giddy one. And we had many happy days together after that, the three of us. Like today, here on this big rock.

"I don't see any snails," said Jimmy. "I want to eat a snail." His voice woke me from my memories.

"It's hard to find a snail at the end of summer," I said.

"Then I want to eat a giant land slug," said Jimmy.

I looked at Jimmy. He was as long as the center of a water lily now and clearly a strong young frog. But he was way too small to be eating the giant slugs. Other frogs don't taste a giant land slug till their mouths are big enough to swallow it whole. But Jimmy knew the taste of slugs, crayfish, and even minnows—all because Pin brought him everything. And he was looking a little bit fat around the middle. "Pin, I really think you ought to stop feeding Jimmy."

Pin didn't answer. I saw his left vocal sac tremble for a moment, as though he thought of croaking. But then it stopped.

"Listen, Pin, he isn't developing the skills he needs to be an ordinary frog. He has to feed himself."

"Jimmy eat good," said Pin.

"Of course he eats good. You know that's not the point."

"I take cayeh of Jimmy," said Pin.

"But that's exactly what's wrong," I said. "He needs to know how to take care of himself. Pin, don't you realize you could get killed at any moment?"

Pin looked at me. "No one ki-y me."

"No one has killed you yet. But it could happen tomorrow. Or an hour from now. Or a second from now. That's the fate of the frog."

Pin shook his head. "Not me. Not De Fawg Pin."

"Oh, you've made a name for yourself, you have. You made the turtle snap at a rock and hurt the tip of his jaw your very first day in the old pond back in the end of April. You confused everyone with that stunt of jumping on the water snake's head in June. The word got around, crazy frog and all that. And it spread from pond to pond until everyone everywhere stayed out of your way. But memories fade. It's September, Pin. You pulled your stunts months ago. Pretty soon some snapping turtle is going to eye those meaty thighs of yours."

"Tuhtuh dumb. I'm not dumb. Tuhtuh not eat me."

"Well, there it is. I knew it. You think you're smarter than every creature in this pond, don't you?"

"Yup," said Pin.

"Well, you're not smarter than the hag."

Jimmy turned pale. "The hag," he whispered.

Pin turned pale.

"See, you're afraid," I said to Pin.

"No," said Pin.

102

"You turned pale," I said. "You're afraid."

"No, Jade," said Pin. "I'm mad. I hate hag."

"Every frog hates the hag. The very thought of her popping you or me or Jimmy into a stew—why, it turns my stomach."

Pin stared at me.

Jimmy stared at me.

I flicked my tongue and swallowed a water spider that should have known better than to come so close. It had a tantalizing, light flavor.

Jimmy lost interest, as froglets do, and focused his eyes on a late-summer snail that was slowly climbing up the broad leaf of a cattail.

But Pin kept staring at me. "Why you tawking about hag now?"

"The new wood frog I met, she told me the hag's been searching around lately down at the end of our pond." I scanned the surface of the water for more stray water spiders. There weren't any.

"No," said Pin. "Hag iv fah away."

"The hag may live far away, near our

old pond, but she's been at this pond just this week. And she seems to be on the lookout for big frogs."

"If hag want fawg, hag can make fawg," said Pin.

"The hag can't make frogs. What ridiculous things you say." I watched a minnow go by and wondered how Pin could enjoy them so much. They looked tough to me. "Anyway, if she gets you, Jimmy will be lost. He won't know how to survive. You have to stop feeding him, so he can learn to take care of himself."

"Jimmy baby."

"How can you say such a silly thing? Jimmy's not a baby! He's a froglet. He's getting bigger by the day."

"Jimmy my baby."

"Well, if you mean it that way, okay. Then he's my baby, too, I guess." I listened to my own words. They sounded foreign. "This isn't natural, all this talk about babies. It isn't froglike. We have to be froglike. I wouldn't feed Jimmy. I wouldn't even know he was my son if he hadn't taken to staying with us."

"But you happy you know him," said Pin.

"Happy I know him?"

"Yup," said Pin.

I looked at Jimmy. He looked up at me with his nicely prominent eyes. His skin was glossy. The raspiness around his mouth, which he used for scraping algae from rocks in his tadpole days, was entirely gone now. I could imagine him in three years' time, a fully mature frog, slimmed down a bit and croaking loudly in the bulrushes. "Yes," I said slowly. "I guess I am happy I know him."

"You uv him," said Pin.

"Uv? I can't understand."

"Uv, uv, uv!" Pin dropped his tongue out of his mouth and mashed it with both forefeet until it was wide and flat with a gully down the center. Then he shaped the tip of it into a point and pushed it back inside his mouth, careful not to change its shape. "You *lll*ove him," said Pin.

I was stunned. "How could I love him? I'm a frog."

Pin blinked.

"Well, I admit it's fun to watch him play leapfrog with the other froglets. But I'd enjoy that even if he wasn't mine."

"Mhmmm," said Pin.

"And it's comforting to sit beside him motionless on our rock in the sun. But, then, it's always nice to have the company of another green frog, no matter who it is."

"Mhmmm," said Pin.

"And..."

The shadow flashed and I leaped. Pin followed me under the water. I looked around. Jimmy. Where was Jimmy? I came up under a lily pad and peeked out just in time to see the hag holding a net in one hand. In the other she held Jimmy by a hind leg.

"You'll grow into a fat one, won't you, froggy?" she said with a dry cackle. "I'm sorry I missed that big guy beside you, but there are others. There are always others." She snorted and a thin smile cracked across her face. "Ha ha ha ha." She tossed Jimmy over her shoulder into a wooden bucket. Then she slammed the lid on the bucket.

CHAPTER NINE

Battle

"Jimmy's a goner," I said. "Here you went and made me uv him, I mean *love* him, and he's gone." I bobbed around under the lily pad.

Pin swam back and forth in front of me, in a worried frenzy. His useless swimming only made things worse.

"Oh, Pin, you are a wretched frog, after all. I thought you had brought me such wonderful things in life. Such odd and new things. And now all you've done is make me sad, and a frog is never supposed to be sad. Oh me, oh me, oh me, oh me."

Pin stopped swimming suddenly. "Don't tawk," he said.

"I can talk all I want," I said. "I'm tired of you making me do things. I listened to you about our mating hole and we almost doomed a thousand tadpoles. And then you had me carrying them in my mouth. And then we *fed* them—who ever heard of a frog feeding tadpoles? And then we carried the few left on our backs. Oh, you've led me into crazy ways. And all because I did what you said. But I won't do it now. I'll shout if I want. I'll scream. Aaaaaa!"

"Don't tawk," said Pin. "I can't ink if you tawk."

"*Ink!* That does it. I'm tired of the stupid way you talk. You had me liking it. But it's just plain stupid. And you blame it on your tongue. You have a perfectly normal froggy tongue. You eat good with it, why can't you talk good with it?"

"Don't tawk," said Pin. "I'm inking."

"You can't *ink*," I screamed. "Frogs don't ink. Squids do."

"Ink," said Pin. "I'm inking about Jim-my."

"Poor little Jimmy," I said.

"Pead don't tawk," said Pin.

"*Please,* the word is *please,* not *pead.* You know, I never told you this, but the wood frog told me not to trust you."

Pin looked at me.

"She said that my curiosity would ruin me. And I know it's true. I've always been too interested in new and different things. Oh me, oh me, oh me, oh me. The wood frog was right."

"I hate wood fawg," said Pin. "Wood fawg bad."

"Wood frogs aren't bad at all. I like this one. How dare you insult her?"

"Wood fawg hide eye," said Pin. "Wood fawg dief."

"You're such a fool. She's not a thief. She just looks like she has a brown mask across her eyes. But it's her coloring, that's all." I looked around. "I wish I could find something to fling across your eyes," I screamed. "I wish I could bang you on the head. I wish I could punch you in the nose!"

"I've got an idea!" shouted Pin. "We get Jimmy."

I stared at him. "We will?"

"Jimmy, Jimmy, Jimmy," shouted a chorus of froglets.

I was so surprised, I gulped water. Pin and I looked around at all the little frogs who had silently surrounded us while we were arguing. I counted. One dozen. Two dozen. Three dozen. Four dozen. And one left over. Forty-nine froglets.

"Who you?" said Pin.

"We're fawgs," they said together.

"They're our children," I said, amazed. "They have to be. These are the froglets we kept safe in the mating hole. I can't believe it." I looked across their happy little faces. "They've all stayed together, ever since we carried them here. Like a family. Like one huge frog family." I thought about it. "It's unfroglike."

"It good," said Pin.

"Good, good, good," said the froglets.

"They're all your children," I said. "They think like you."

"We're fawgs," screamed the froglets. "We want Jimmy."

"Don't tawk," said Pin. "I tawk. I have an idea." He stared at the froglets. They stared back. Then he turned to me. "I take hag away. You knock de bucket. De bucket faw. Jimmy get out."

"Hurrah!" shouted the froglets. "The bucket will fall over. Jimmy will be free. Hurrah!"

"How can I knock over that big, heavy bucket?" I said.

"Get de wood fawg to hep you."

"Frogs don't help each other," I said.

"Get de wood fawg. Go!"

"But how will you take the hag away?"

"I've got an idea. Go," said Pin. He turned to the froglets. "You act good now. Hide in de weed. Don't get eaten."

"Lot of good that'll do," I said. "Froglets never obey."

Pin looked back at me. "Go!"

I hesitated. I had lost my sweet son Jimmy and now maybe I was about to lose my husband. I couldn't bear the thought. "Be careful," I whispered.

Pin nodded. "Good-bye, Jade."

I swam to the mud far behind the hag and looked around for the wood frog. I hopped in and out of the undergrowth. But she was nowhere to be found. I sighed. It didn't really matter, though. If I had asked the wood frog to help me, she'd have thought I was crazy.

Pin swam in the other direction, right toward where the hag had been. I could see his eyes and nose bobbing in the water. He looked every which way for her. But the hag wasn't standing on the muddy bank anymore. Her net was still there—but she was gone.

Pin came out onto the mud and sat very still. I knew he was trying to sense her motions through vibrations in the mud.

I leaped toward the bucket, which was now halfway between us. If Pin and I were fast enough, we could free Jimmy before the hag reappeared.

A sharp ray of amber light caught my eye. It was the sun reflecting off the hag's crystal ring as she came flying out of the overhanging willow branches. She landed

with a thud, scooping me up in her bare hand with one swift grab. I knew I was a dead frog.

"Croak!" shouted Pin. "Croak, croak, croak!"

The hag spun around and saw Pin do a flip in the air. "Aha! The big guy again. That juicy, fat, oversize guy." She crept toward the bucket. "Let me just drop this froggy into the bucket and then you're next, big guy."

"Croak!" shouted Pin. He leaped right toward the hag. "Croak! Croak!"

The hag cackled. "Well, look at that. A froggy that croaks with only one vocal sac. A sick froggy. Probably can't hop too far. Ha ha ha ha. An easy froggy to catch."

"Croak!" shouted Pin. He leaped toward her again. Then he suddenly turned and leaped away quickly. "Croak, croak, croak."

"Hey, wait a minute, big guy." The hag looked from me to Pin. "He's worth three of you!" She dropped me on the mud and picked up her net.

Pin stopped hopping.

I had to get to Jimmy right away. I tried to leap and fell flat on my belly. I couldn't move my hind legs, the hag had squeezed them so hard. Helpless, I watched Pin and the hag.

The hag crept toward Pin slowly. She swung her net. She had aimed perfectly.

Pin leaped backward at the last second.

I'd never seen a frog leap backward! The net slapped down on the mud in front of Pin.

"Croak," said Pin.

"You hopped backward," said the hag, with as much surprise as I felt. "Frogs can't do that!" Then her voice rose in anger. "Think I can't get you, is that it? Well, I'll get you, my amphibious morsel. I'll get you." She lifted her net slowly.

I forced my right hind leg out in a stretch. And yes, oh yes, it was working now. I tried my left. It stayed cramped. Panic clutched me. I stared at Pin and the hag.

This time the net came down about five inches behind where Pin had been sitting. But Pin leaped at the last minute—to the side.

"A sideways leap!" The hag leaned over and stuck her bumpy chin out at Pin. She snorted. "An acrobat frog, is that what you think you are? Well, I can handle that!" She looked around.

She marched right past me to a clump of chamomile growing on the bank beside the wooden bucket that held our Jimmy prisoner. She plucked the chamomile. "A little herbal boost will make my net big. I'll catch you in an instant." She stuck the plant in her mouth and chewed like a cow. Then she held the net in front of her and spit a huge gob of muck onto it. The net immediately grew three times bigger.

The hag raised it over her head and swung hard. The net caught on a hawthorn branch and ripped.

"Beastly thing," she shouted. She left the net dangling from the branch and clenched her fists. She rubbed her crystal ring and thought for a moment. "All right, froggy, no more fooling around. It's time for serious magic."

She walked toward Pin very slowly, holding her glowing amber crystal at chest level, pointed right at him. She rubbed the crystal with a circular motion. "Ice, froggy. What do you think of that? Nice ice to make your cold blood slow to a stop. Ha ha ha ha."

And suddenly a glistening wall of ice rose up behind Pin. "It's so high, you can't jump over it. It's so slippery, you can't climb it. Ha ha ha ha. It's behind you, froggy. You can't jump backward. Ha ha ha ha." She rubbed her ring again. "It's on both sides of you, froggy. You can't jump sideways. Ha ha ha ha." And the ice wall rose up on both sides of Pin. The hag put her hand on her ring to rub again. "It's—"

But before she could say it, Pin leaped and landed right on the hag's face, grabbing hold of her nose.

"Owwww!" screamed the hag. The air was a blur of hag fingers and frog legs. Suddenly the hag's crystal ring went flying off her finger and into the mud.

"Get Jimmy," Pin shouted to me.

"Who's Jimmy?" screamed the hag as she snorted and flailed around. She pulled fiercely at Pin. But he held on to her nose just like he held on to my belly when we mated. The strength of his grip was astounding.

I stretched my left thigh in desperation. It finally worked again! I leaped to the bucket and jumped against it.

It rocked a little and then came to a halt.

"High," shouted Pin. "Hit it high."

I jumped high and smashed into the bucket a few inches under the rim.

It rocked on its bottom edge, then slammed to a halt again.

"High, high, high," shouted Pin.

"High?" screamed the hag. "What do you mean, you infernal frog?" She was holding him by both hind legs and pulling as hard as she could. Her snorts were now as loud as the bugle of a moose.

I looked at that heavy wooden bucket and felt defeated. It was enormous, and I was but one little green frog. But Jimmy was inside. I could hear him leaping about. I jumped with all the strength I had left and slammed against the rim of the bucket. At the same moment that I slammed against it, forty-nine little froglets came slamming up against it, too.

It crashed over on its side, and the lid rolled away.

"Jimmy," I called.

A crowd of froglets went leaping past me and splashed into the water. I leaped in

after them, grateful for the notorious dis-
obedience of froglets that had made them
not stay hidden in the weeds as Pin had
ordered.

CHAPTER TEN

The Bullfrog

Jimmy and I and the forty-nine little
froglets sat on the bottom of the pond. We
closed our nostrils and waited. Our goggle-
like eyelids kept out the water but still let
us see the underwater world.

The protozoa streaked the water with
green and red. The brown and white hy-
dras floated around us, dangling their ten-
tacles. The bristle worms crawled over our
toes, nibbling up the debris off the bottom.
A great diving beetle plunged down near

Jimmy, snapped up a hydra, then darted away. The life of the pond went on as if things were normal. But nothing was normal for us anymore. Pin was gone.

A bullfrog swam near and eyed us.

"We belong to Pin," I shouted.

The bullfrog came closer.

"Pin," I shouted, "the giant green frog that baffles snapping turtles and zaps water snakes. This is De Fawg Pin's family."

The bullfrog hesitated.

"You don't want to know what De Fawg Pin can do to bullfrogs," I said in a steely voice.

The bullfrog muttered, "Frog family? Who ever heard of a frog family?" He swam on by.

We waited for hours. The water darkened. I stayed attentive, but I knew the sun's rays were going down. I knew it soon would be too dark to see predators. The children and I would be forced to go up to the surface. It was time to face the fact that Pin was gone forever. "Children," I said, working to keep my voice from cracking with sadness, "children, I have bad news."

"About Daddy?" said Jimmy.

Daddy. The word pierced my heart. Pin had taught Jimmy to call him Daddy. "Yes." I stayed silent for a long moment. Then I looked around at all their expectant faces. "The hag got Daddy."

"I don't believe it," said Jimmy. "Daddy's too smart."

"Sometimes even smart frogs get caught."

"Daddy's not a frog, he's a fawg," said Jimmy.

"We're all fawgs," said the froglets. "No hag can hurt a fawg."

"Last time I saw him," I said, "the hag was holding on to him by both hind legs."

"No," said Jimmy. "De Fawg Pin lives. I know it."

"De Fawg Pin lives," screamed the froglets.

"De Fawg Pin," I said slowly. "Poor lost Pin."

The same bullfrog that had bothered us three or four hours ago came swimming back. "Oh, that Pin," he said. "What a frog. Oh boy, do I love what happened tonight! Yeah, that was good. Heh heh heh."

Oh me, oh me, oh me, oh me. Pin was dead for sure. Now there was nothing to threaten the bullfrog with. I tensed for the fight.

"Guess what I ate for supper," said the bullfrog. "Go on, guess."

I thought of what must remain of Pin after the hag pulled his legs off. For a moment I cursed the fatal strength of a healthy frog's mating grip. Then I sighed. Such is

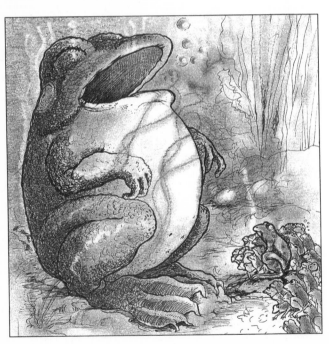

the way of the world. My Pin had been ripped apart and some of him was now in the belly of this hideous bullfrog.

"Want a hint?" said the bullfrog. "Cold blood and mucky mucus. Heh heh heh."

I thought of Pin's lovely shiny skin, so slick from his mucus glands. "A pox on you," I shouted at the bullfrog.

"Heh heh," said the bullfrog. "Very fitting. Want another hint?" He snickered. "Strange noises."

I thought of Pin's funny way of talking. I would never hear the word *uv* again. My whole being ached. "You cannibal," I said with cold hatred. "You despicable cannibal."

The bullfrog bobbed around us. The froglets huddled together. "Drippy and delicious," said the bullfrog in his raspy voice. "Zingy. A real treat for my froggy palate."

"You're not a frog," shouted Jimmy, "you're a toad. You're a big old toad disguised as a stupid old bullfrog."

Calling a frog a toad was the worst insult imaginable. I was astounded at Jimmy's courage. He was Pin's son, all right.

"Heh heh heh." The bullfrog opened his mouth and swallowed a swarm of protozoa. "Don't panic, froglet. I didn't steal it. Pin threw it away."

"What?" I said.

"What, what, what?" chorused the froglets.

The bullfrog swam right up to me. He swayed back and forth. "He kept screaming *jade*. What's that mean, *jade?*"

"Jade," I said softly.

The bullfrog hiccuped. A stream of bubbles went up from his mouth. "You know, for a frog that can rip the nose right off a witch, that Pin doesn't know squat." He shut his eyes and said dreamily, "It was succulent, too." Then he opened his eyes wide and thrust his face in mine. "Pin doesn't even know that frogs can sit underwater and breathe through their skins. He didn't know this is where you'd be, when anyone knows a frog goes straight to the bottom and waits when there's danger."

The bullfrog gulped in another swarm of

protozoa. "He's been hopping around frantically, looking for you like a mother bird or a mammal or something. Oh, that maniac Pin. I've been laughing for hours." The bullfrog belched.

"Where is he now?" I asked.

The bullfrog stared at me. "You want to find him as much as he wants to find you, don't you?" He looked around at the froglets. "You all want to, don't you? What's going on? Since when do frogs care what happens to other frogs?"

"Where is he?" I said.

The bullfrog's look of amazement was replaced quickly by a sly look. "What'll you give me if I tell you?"

"Go eat a witch's nose," shouted Jimmy. "Let's go find him, Mamma." He shot up through the water. All the froglets followed.

I climbed up onto our granite rock, leaving the froglets suspended in the water, their bulging eyes taking in everything. There sat Pin, in the middle of the rock, his back to us, croaking sadly with his left vocal sac.

"Pin," I said.

Pin jumped around. "Jade, my Jade." His mouth dropped open, and his tongue flopped onto the rock. I scooped it up and gently put it back in his mouth. "Jimmy?" he said.

"He's here," I said. "They're all here. All fifty of them."

He looked around at the froglets, and his eyes showed peace and happiness.

The froglets climbed onto the surrounding lily pads. "Night, Daddy. Night, Mamma," they said.

Pin and I sat on the warm rock, with Jimmy between us, and watched the moon grow gibbous in that wonderful sky.

CHAPTER ELEVEN

Back to the Well

The sun was out in full glare. The children were leaping for their breakfast here and there. I had just swallowed a big horsefly. The morning seemed off to a terrific start, when Pin made his announcement.

"Back," said Pin. "We go back."

"Back?" I said. Then I brightened. "Back to our old pond?"

"No," said Pin. "Back to de...de...oh, I can't day it."

"You can't say it. All right. Does it have *rrrr* or *ssss* or *thhhh* in it?"

"No."

"Does it have *llll?*"

"Yup," said Pin.

"All right, is *llll* at the beginning or the end of the word?"

"End," said Pin. "At de beginning *we.*"

"We-llll," I said. "The well. What's the well?"

"De weyeh ow mating hoe."

"Our mating hole is called a well?"

"Yup. Dat what human caw it."

I looked at Pin with admiration. All the frogs I talked to admired me for knowing so much about the world. But Pin knew all sorts of things I'd never heard of. Still, what he was saying right now didn't make me happy. "We're going back there? Why on earth should we go back to the well?"

"No hag," said Pin.

"But there's no hag here either anymore," I said. "You took her nose off. She won't come back."

"Hag come back," said Pin. "Hag come back and take fawg." He looked out over our frolicking froglets. "Hag eat aw de fawg."

"No," I said. "She's afraid of you now. Anyway, if she comes back, you can pull off her ears!"

"We go," said Pin. "Now." He leaped into the water and swam to the bank. He croaked his loudest. "Come, fawg! We go now."

A crowd of froglets swam to the bank and leaped out into the grasses.

"This is insane," I said. "We can't all live in the well. Where will we find food? How will we all swim about? It's a terrible idea."

But no one was listening.

I watched the bodies of my dozens of children hop through the grasses after their father, and I felt something I'd never felt before. It was a warmth that made my chest swell. It was pride. Yes, I would follow that crazy frog and all those crazy froglets. I would follow them, and we would find a way to survive. I didn't know how, but I knew we would.

The trip took a little longer than usual,

because the froglets weren't accustomed to land travel. When we were finally close to the well, we heard a dreadful noise: the discordant voice of a human. I jumped onto a rotten log and looked around for the hag.

Pin spied the source of the voice faster than I did. "A woman," he said.

I followed his eyes. A young human woman with great gobs of hair, a green lace dress, and something small and sparkly on her head was sitting in the grass by the well. She sang loudly. It sounded awful to my frog ears.

"Petty ong," said Pin.

I listened more closely. There was nothing pretty at all about her song. "You have unusual taste," I said.

Pin looked at me. Then he looked back at the human woman.

This human woman annoyed me. I didn't like the odd way Pin looked at her. "What do we do now?"

"We wait," said Pin. "De woman go."

"Wait," said the froglets, as they leaped forward toward the well. "Wait."

"But you're not waiting," I shouted after them. "Come back here right now. Humans are dangerous. Remember the hag. Come back."

The froglets continued their leaping. "She's green. She can't be all bad," they screamed. "Our well, our well, our well."

The first to reach the well was Jimmy. He hopped up on the well wall.

"Oooo," said the human woman. She stood up beside the well. "What a cunning little frog." She leaned her face toward Jimmy.

"She's going to eat him," I said. "Oh, Pin, she's going to eat him."

"No," said Pin. "A woman not eat fawg. A woman cook fawg, den eat fawg."

"No," I screamed. "Don't let her cook Jimmy."

Pin leaped through the grasses toward the well with me by his side.

By now the human woman held Jimmy in her hand and stood back, watching the other froglets go diving down into the well. "My goodness," she said. "It's a frog invasion." She leaned over the well. "One, two, three, four…why, there must be twenty frogs here. And they're still coming!" She cupped her hand over Jimmy and walked back to her spot in the grass. She sat down.

She lifted her top hand off Jimmy. "There now, frog, don't hop off. You're the most beautiful green I've ever seen. Let's be friends."

Jimmy didn't move.

The human woman laughed. "The idea of being friends with a frog! How foolish I

sound." She lifted Jimmy up, level with her face.

Pin and I were a leap away from her now. "Oh," I whispered to Pin. "She's going to put him in her mouth. She's going to eat him after all."

"No," said Pin firmly. "De woman not eat Jimmy."

The human woman spoke in a singsong. "Funny little frog. Dandy little frog. Let me take a closer look at you." Her glistening red lips parted slightly. Her big white teeth showed.

"She is going to eat him!" I said. "She is, she is!"

"No!" Pin shook his head. "No."

"Well, if she's not going to eat him, what's she doing with him?"

"I don't know," said Pin. "Maybe woman want pet."

The human woman sighed. "I wish..." She shut her eyes and closed her hand once again over Jimmy. Then she brought her hands closer to her face. "I wish..." Her lips trembled.

"She's going to eat him," I screamed.

"No." Pin shook his head again, but I could see doubt spring into his eyes. "No, it can't be." His voice was worried.

The human woman brought her hands all the way up, so they were touching her lips.

"Now," I said to Pin. "Save him now, Pin, or he's gone forever!"

Just as the human woman's hands reached her face, Pin leaped into them, knocking Jimmy off with one big swat of his foreleg. Pin met her lips as Jimmy fell away and landed at my feet. She opened her eyes. "Oooooo!" she screamed, jumping backward.

I gasped.

There in front of the human woman was a tall, naked human man.

"Oooooo!" screamed the human woman.

The human man looked down at his nakedness. "Aaaaaa!" he screamed. He leaped behind the well.

"Who are you?" said the human woman.

"De Fawg Pin," said the human man.

Well, I got mad at that. What nerve! He was nothing like my beautiful Pin. Oh, where was my beautiful Pin?

"What?" said the human woman.

The human man looked dazed. "I…" He looked around helplessly. Then he said slowly, "I'm a prince."

"Oh." The human woman's voice got weak. "I don't see how… oh… I mean…" She wrung her hands. "Oh." Her face went pale. She looked back at the human man. "You're a very handsome prince," she whispered, "even if you are a dream. I'm a princess. But, then, you must know that, since you're part of my dream."

"Look, could you get me some clothes?" said the human man.

The human woman bit her bottom lip. "You sound real. I mean, wanting clothes, that's real."

"I'm every bit as real as you are," said the human man.

"Oh dear," said the human woman. "Really? I thought I was imagining you. Oh dear." Her face turned red. "Oh dear."

"Clothes," said the human man.

"Yes, of course," said the human woman. "Yes." She turned around, then she spun back with both hands on her cheeks. "But where did you come from? Who are you? I mean, how…?"

"I'm just as confused as you are," said the human man.

The human woman dropped her hands. "You're really real?"

"Really real."

She smiled shyly. Then she ran off toward the palace, looking back over her shoulder every few seconds. "Don't go away. I'll be right back," she called.

I couldn't make sense of this human conversation, and I was frantic about Pin. "Pin," I shouted, leaping about. "Pin, Pin, where are you?"

The human man looked in my direction, but I sat so still that I knew he couldn't see me. "Jade, is that you? Is that my frog wife?"

I was shocked. This human man was obviously completely mad. Dangerous. Where

had he heard my name? "Children," I shouted. "All of you, come right now. We're going back to the pond. Now."

"But where's Daddy?" screamed the froglets from inside the well. "We want Daddy. What's happened to our daddy?"

"Come now!" I shouted in a tone so commanding that one by one the worried froglets leaped to the top of the well in uncustomary obedience and came to me in the grass.

The human man reached out his hands toward the froglets. I thought he was going to catch them. But he didn't touch them. He merely reached out his hands and sighed. "Good-bye, my little froglets. Good-bye, my sweet children." He looked toward the grass with searching eyes. "Good-bye, frog wife. Best possible wife. I love you. Try to remember me. Good-bye, good-bye."

I looked at him, alone and naked, so sad, with such longing in his voice. He stared straight at me now. There was something vaguely familiar about his golden brown eyes.

I searched through the grasses one last

time for Pin. "Pin," I called as loud as I could. "Pin, where are you?"

"Where's Daddy?" screamed the froglets, in bunches all around me. "Where's Daddy? Where's Daddy?"

"Pin, Pin," I called. Where was my Pin? I thought of all the crazy days we had spent together. I thought of Pin learning to swim and learning to eat and learning to croak. I thought of Pin beating the snapping turtle and the water snake and the hag. I thought of Pin carrying tadpoles in his mouth and naming me Jade. He had brought so many wonderful changes to my life. I wanted Pin with me again. I wanted all those days that should have stretched out ahead of us. Days of Pin saying extraordinary things and doing extraordinary things. Days of happiness and adventure. Days of love.

"Mamma," came the insistent chorus of froglets, "where's Daddy?"

I shook my head in bewilderment.

"I know," said Jimmy.

I looked at Jimmy.

Jimmy looked long at the human man.

Then he turned to the rest of us. "He disappeared."

I looked from Jimmy to the human man. He was watching us. He acted like he was listening. His face was grief-stricken.

Somehow in that very moment I knew that Pin was gone forever. Jimmy was right—Pin had disappeared. I felt the strangest sensation of my life: A tear rolled down my cheek.

"Croak," said Jimmy in a tiny voice.

I looked at him. "Jimmy, you just croaked. For the very first time. Do it again."

Jimmy croaked a little louder. His left vocal sac inflated and deflated.

"I can croak, too," said another froglet. He croaked. His left vocal sac inflated and deflated.

"Me too," shouted another.

And the air was filled with croaks, as left vocal sacs inflated and deflated all around me.

"We'll be okay," said Jimmy. "We can protect ourselves. We can work together. We can help each other."

"Frogs don't help each other," I said automatically.

"But fawgs do," said Jimmy.

I looked at the hopeful little faces of my froglets. "Yes," I said. "Fawgs do."